RABBITS

and Their Night-Time Habits

The Amusing Adventures of Missy and Mr. Bun
by Claire Sells

Published by Claire Sells
(c) Claire Sells 2016

ISBN: 978-1-5262-0155-3

Foreword:
I was going through a particularly rough time in my life last year, when driving over the downs, I happened to look up at the sky. I was amused by what I saw, a bunny cloud complete with a pair of rabbity ears. If that wasn't a sign to create this book, I don't know what was!

Did you know that rabbits are most lively at night? So, when we are all fast asleep and the sky is dark and full of stars, whilst the moon softly shines and we are warm in our beds, those naughty little rabbits, get up to all kinds of things!

Have you any idea or thought as such, that our dear little furry friends get up to so much? Here in this book all will be revealed, of Missy and Mr. Bun's night-time habits!

Missy decided she would have a relaxing bath, with bubbles and soap and all the nice stuff!

he bunnies were having a
ncy dress party, so Missy
ore a hat made with fruit!

Mr. Bun was sweeping up,
but little did he know
that Missy was hiding in
the leaves!

Mr. Bun decided to invite over his friend Dale, they discussed the world news over some plates of hay.

It was so wet one night that the bunnies each wore a raincoat and decided to set sail in their newly built boat!

Mr. Bun decided to have an Easter egg hunt in the garden. Off they went, wearing an Easter bonnet and with a hoppity skip, to find some eggs that had been well hid!*

Mr. Bun decided to have a disco on a lovely summers night. He put up a glittery ball and the hutch was filled with sparkling light.

It was the night of Halloween,
so the rabbits bobbed for apples,
what a scream!

Those are pretty
fireworks but they
scare us silly!
So we are having a
cosy night in with
some ear muffs and a
bit of light reading!

At the stroke of midnight the rabbits
decided to go for a drive,
and looked up at the stars that shone
brightly in the summer nights sky.

The rabbits decided to hitch a ride on Santa's sleigh, but caused lots of mischief and Santa was nearly delayed!

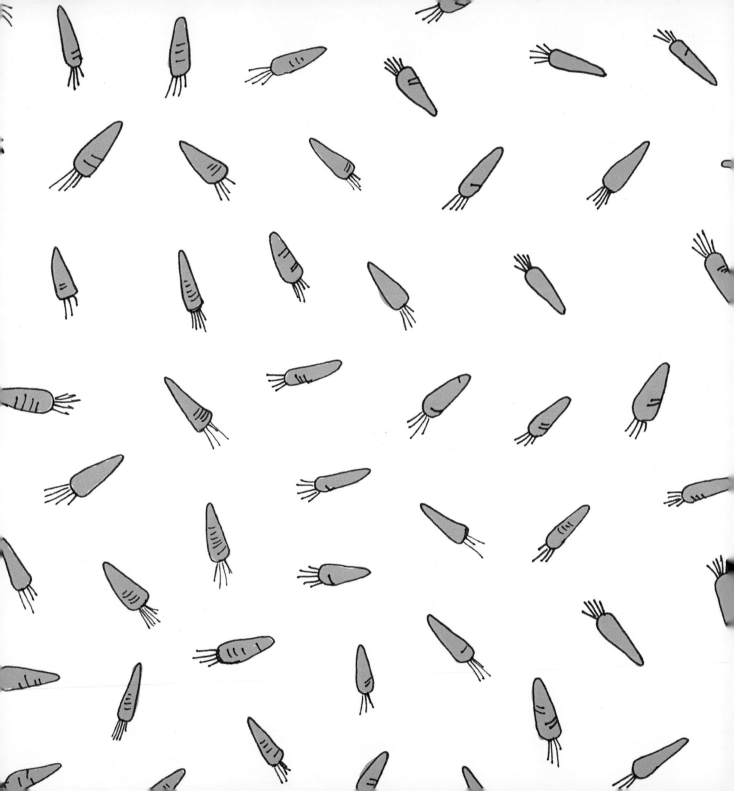